My Little Redheaded Sister

By Christy Lee
Illustrated By Paris Juliana

This book is dedicated to my two daughters, McCall and Marli, who are beautiful, talented, and kind; they fill my life with joy and laughter! And to my own little redheaded sister, Tisha, who has always made my life easier and way more fun. I don't know what I'd do without you!
- Christy Lee

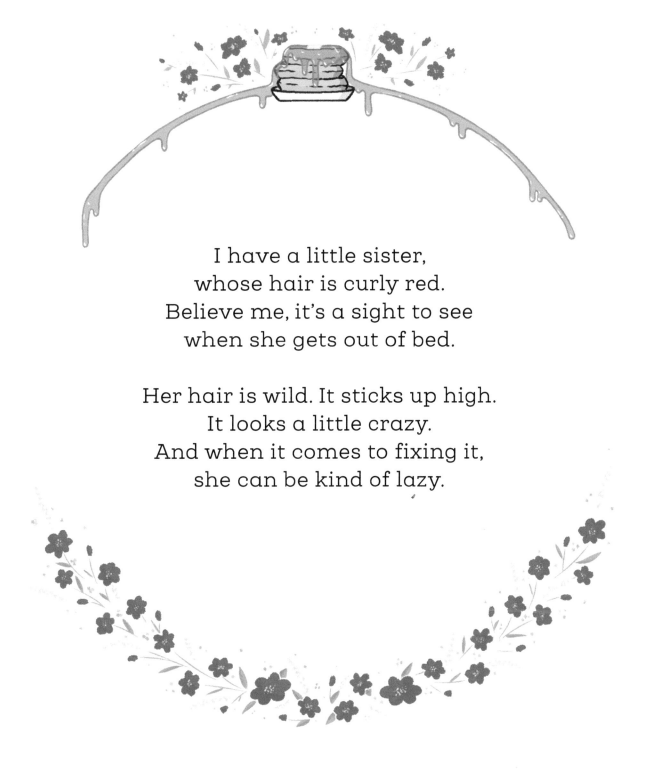

I have a little sister,
whose hair is curly red.
Believe me, it's a sight to see
when she gets out of bed.

Her hair is wild. It sticks up high.
It looks a little crazy.
And when it comes to fixing it,
she can be kind of lazy.

She never likes to mess with things
like bows or rubber bands.
In fact, sometimes, to fix it,
she smooths it with her hands.

My mom attempts to tame it,
at least to say she tried.
But she always pulls it out
as soon as she steps outside.

You would think she'd be embarrassed,
but she doesn't even care.
Because it seems wherever she goes,
people love her crazy hair!

It doesn't matter where we go
or what we end up doing.
As soon as people see her,
they all start ahh and oohing.

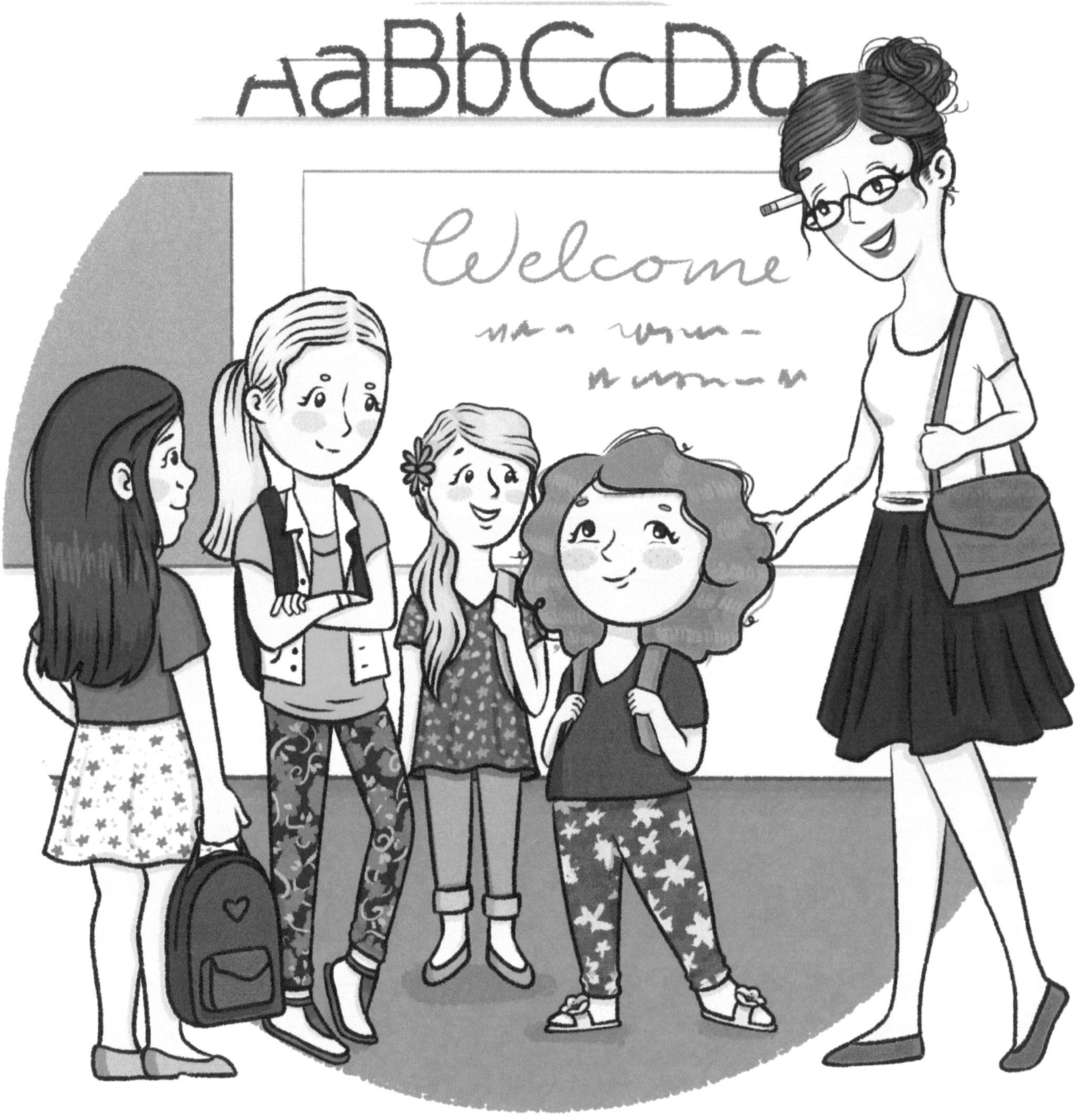
Welcome

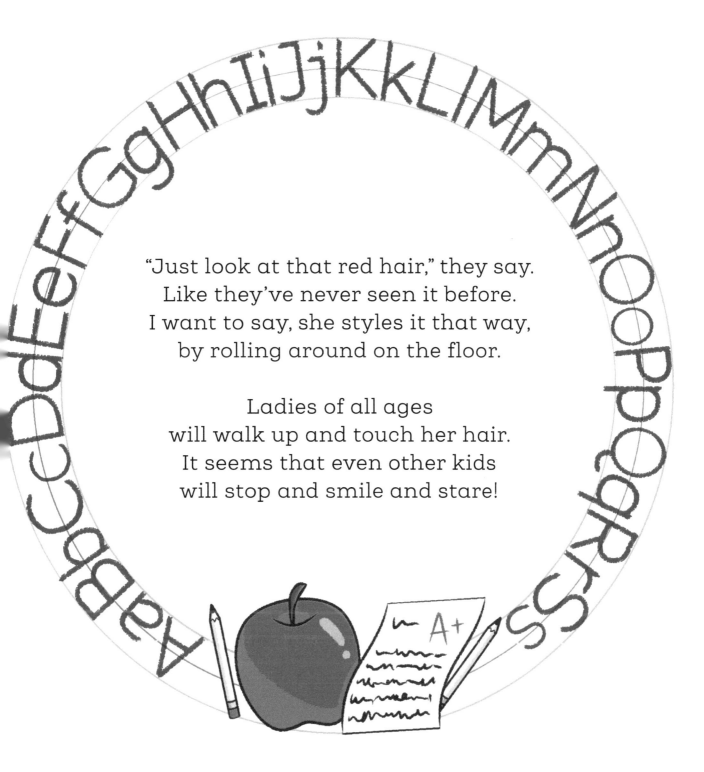

"Just look at that red hair," they say.
Like they've never seen it before.
I want to say, she styles it that way,
by rolling around on the floor.

Ladies of all ages
will walk up and touch her hair.
It seems that even other kids
will stop and smile and stare!

They almost always tell her
that she's such a lucky girl,
to have that beautiful shade of red, and all those
natural curls.

Through the years, we've gotten used to all the
attention and such.
And even I don't roll my eyes,
nearly half as much.

We have a friend named Grandma M,
who we all love a ton.
She also thinks that bright red hair
is cute and so much fun.

The thing I like about Grandma M,
besides being sweet and witty,
she happens to think that straight blond hair is
every bit as pretty!

Every time we see her,
she always goes on and on,
about how amazing it is
that my hair is straight and blond.

I've learned we all have different ways
that we stand out and shine.
We each have special talents.
My sister has hers, and I have mine.

I like to draw and sing and run.
I also love to dance.
And just this year, I think that I
will give ballet a chance.

My sister plays the violin
and just started piano too.
She also thinks that tennis
is something she might want to do.

Yes, my sister and I are different,
but I don't really care.
Even though it draws less attention,
I like my straight blonde hair.

We do have some things in common.
In some ways, we're kind of the same.
We like to eat ice cream and pizza
and make up silly dances and games.

No one makes me laugh like she does,
especially when we've stayed up too late.
And getting woken up early
is something that both of us hate.

But even though we sometimes fight,
I still love her a lot.
Even with all that crazy red hair,
she's the only sister I've got!

Christy Lee lives in a small town in Arizona. She has loved raising her five children in a home that has been in her husband's family for five generations. Christy has written poems about life and the people she loves for over 30 years. She enjoys running in the morning with friends for therapy and hiking, kayaking, and paddle boarding with her husband and kids for fun.

Paris Juliana was born and raised in Arizona. She's been drawing ever since she can remember and, as a self-taught artist, has always had aspirations for a career in art. My Little Redheaded Sister is her first project as a professional illustrator, and she had a great time getting to know the girls and incorporating their personalities into the illustrations.

CPSIA information can be obtained
at www.ICGtesting.com
Printed in the USA
BVHW021220200821
614842BV00021B/135